MAX MADNESS

AND THE SMARTY PANTS SERUM

BY
MARKEEM KENDALL

Tilte: Max Madness and the Smarty Pants Serum
Author: Markeem Kendall

ISBN: 979-8-88992-846-1 (Paperback)

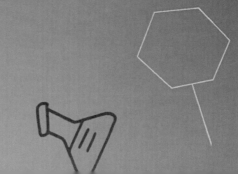

"Wherever there's life...
there's Madness."

- Markeem Kendall,
Founder/CEO of Mark Madness Enterprises

On a muggy Monday in the middle of May, the one and only Max Madness is holed up in his lab tipping and tossing test tubes to the left and right.

Hes got beakers on the table and bowls on the floor. A mixture by the millimeter, a medley by the mile. All of this to perfect his most creative concoction yet.

With his wide-rimmed glasses and dozens of crumpled notepads, Max is determined to produce an excellent elixir, a truly terrific tonic.

He likes to call it his Smarty Pants Serum.

This particular potion has the power to enhance the common cranium. With a dash of wit and a drop of empathy, Max Madness has found a way to improve the quality of the mind, to tweak it and tease it, to make it courteous and kind.

"It's not going to work," his henchmen squawks into his ear. Absalom Jerome Reid, or AJ, or "my mother's sister's boy," as Max likes to call him, has been Max's minion of mad science for quite some time.

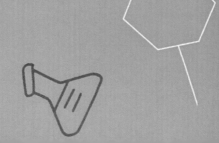

Last spring, the two of them
built a tunnel
between Max's basement lab and
AJ's house. They spend every
weekend, each
Summer, and the hours after
school bustling back and forth,
up and down the tunnel together
working on their
experiments.

The boys hover over the table as the serum bubbles in its beaker. Max sprinkles and trickles a few more ingredients into the batch before giving it a good swirl. It sizzles and pops, pluming a cloud of purple smoke in the air.

"I've done it!" Max shouts, lifting the beaker to the light. "My Smarty Pants Serum is complete."

"It won't work," says his mother's sister's boy, "It's not going to work."

"Sure it will!" Max counters with a grin. He gives the beaker a good shake and pours the mixture into a tube. "We just have to test it out first."

The next morning, Max slips the serum into his backpack as the bus hustles down the block. He's on the sidewalk by the time it screeches to a stop.

AJ comes stumbling up behind him and the pair climbs onto the bus together. Max takes a deep breath and keeps his head down as he makes his way through the first few rows.

At home, in his lab, Max is a mad scientist. A genius, a mastermind, a wiz, but the second he goes to the neighborhood park, the main street candy shop, or even worse, school, Max is just another geek for the popular kids to mock.

They call him "Mad Max" or "Crazy Pants," the popular kids don't believe he's smart at all. The worst of them is Johnny Envy, captain of the soccer team.

Unfortunately, soccer balls aren't the only thing that Johnny likes to kick. He swings his foot into Max's things whenever he gets the chance. In the chemistry lab, on the playground, and even at the school's science fair. Johnny Envy is always toppling something over.

Max and AJ make it all the way to school without Johnny teasing them. When the bus pulls up to the doors, everyone piles out, pushing and rushing inside before the bell rings.

The boys make it all the way to their lockers before they hear the dreaded sound of heavy footsteps coming right toward them. "Well if it isn't Mad Max and his silly sidekick," Johnny sneers.

Johnny reaches for Max's backpack and yanks it out of his arms. He throws it onto the ground and with one swift kick, hurls it right into the hallway wall.

"Leave me alone, Johnny," Max growls, "Or I'll-"

"You'll what?" Johnny bites back, towering over Max. "What will you do?"

Max shivers a little and backs down. "Nothing," he whispers.

"That's what I thought," Johnny sneers, and stomps away with his friends.

Max rushes over to his backpack and unzips one of the pouches, "The serum is safe," he says.

"I'm tired of getting picked on by Johnny Envy," Max declares. "All of this bullying ends, today."

"How are you going to do that?" AJ asks.

"I told you our serum needs to be tested. I think Johnny should be our first subject."

"It's not going to work," AJ says with a shake of his head.

"It will," Max says, "You'll see."

During recess, the boys slip into the locker room while everyone else plays on the field. AJ is Max's lookout at the window while Max shuffles through Johnny's locker.

He tosses Johnny's stuff around until he finds his water bottle at the bottom of the bag.

"Everyone's coming!" AJ whispers, "Hurry up!"

Max pops the top off of the serum and pours it into Johnny's bottle. He gives it a good shake before everyone makes it back to the locker room.

Johnny Envy marches into the room and heads straight for the water bottle. Max and AJ watch with wide eyes as he takes a swig.

He shivers a little and shakes a bit. His eyes flash purple before he's back to normal again. Then something strange happens. Johnny looks right at Max and smiles. "Hey there, my friend!" Johnny says, "We've got art class together after this. Want to walk with me?"

"S-Sure," Max stutters and drags AJ by the wrist as they follow Johnny out of the room.

Johnny Envy is the school's new genius; and he's not just smart, he's nice.

He helps Penelope Parker pick up her pencils and Holly Hanover hold her lunch tray.

He knows all the answers to every question in class, but he raises his hand before he speaks. He says "please" and "thank you," and the occasional "excuse me." Max can't believe it, he really achieved it.

The Smarty Pants Serum is a success.

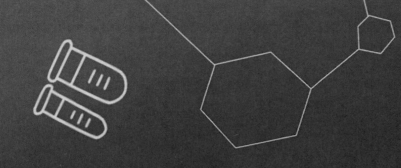

Max decides to do one final test to see if Johnny Envy is completely cured of his carelessness. When Johnny walks down the hallway at the end of the school day, Max drops his backpack on the floor.

He wants to see if Johnny will kick it like he did that morning.

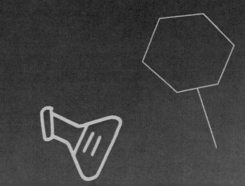

When Johnny sees the
backpack, he stoops down to
scoop it up. "Max-A-Million!"

he says with a grin, "I think you
dropped this."

Max returns the smile and
reaches for the backpack,
"Thank you, my friend-"

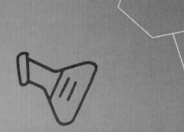

Suddenly, Johnny shivers a little and shakes a bit. His eyes flash purple, and his grin drops to a frown. "What are you smiling at, Crazy Pants?" he says, hurling Max's backpack against the wall.

As Johnny Envy walks away, Max waits for the sadness to come. He tries to get frustrated or angry, but all he can seem to do is smile.

"Why are you smiling?" AJ asks, handing Max his backpack.

"My Smarty Pants serum is a success!" Max giggles in delight, "It wasn't permanent, but that doesn't matter. We just have to find a way to make it last longer. To the lab!"

AJ races out of the The backs of
two boys school doors after Max.
"It's not going to work!"
He shouts.

"Oh, it will," Max replies as they sprint into the sunshine.

"I'm Max Madness. I can do anything!"

MEET THE AUTHOR

Markeem Kendall, Founder/CEO of Mark Madness Enterprises is the epitome of the young person's dream, knocking down closed doors while opening up new doors for other dreamers in the process!

Born in 1977, Kendall a South Philadelphia native showed ambition early on in life. This ambition was never dampened by the harsh nature of his environment. Dropping out of high school his senior year to support his family, Kendall never lost sight of his dream: a career in entertainment.

Mark Madness Enterprises is a parent holding company based out of Philadelphia, PA which began its ascension in 1998 with Mark Madness Entertainment. Over the course of the past thirteen years, Mark Madness Enterprises has evolved to include the following subsidiaries: Madness Designs, The Waterview Lounge, Madness Studios, Kendall Properties & Stop the Madness Foundation (STMF) a 501(c)3 non-profit organization.

Made in United States
North Haven, CT
23 May 2023

36895709R00033